Florence W. Snedeker

A Family Canoe Trip

Volume 1

Florence W. Snedeker

A Family Canoe Trip
Volume 1

ISBN/EAN: 9783337144821

Printed in Europe, USA, Canada, Australia, Japan

Cover: Foto ©Andreas Hilbeck / pixelio.de

More available books at **www.hansebooks.com**

A FAMILY CANOE TRIP

BY

FLORENCE WATTERS SNEDEKER

ILLUSTRATED

NEW YORK

HARPER & BROTHERS, FRANKLIN SQUARE

1892

OTHER VOLUMES IN

Harper's "Black and White" Series.

Illustrated. 32mo, Cloth, 50 cents each.

A LITTLE SWISS SOJOURN. By WILLIAM DEAN HOW-
ELLS. (*In Press.*)

A LETTER OF INTRODUCTION. A Farce. By WILLIAM
DEAN HOWELLS.

JAMES RUSSELL LOWELL. An Address. By GEORGE
WILLIAM CURTIS.

IN THE VESTIBULE LIMITED. By BRANDER MAT-
THEWS.

THE ALBANY DEPOT. A Farce. By WILLIAM DEAN
HOWELLS.

PUBLISHED BY HARPER & BROTHERS, NEW YORK.

*For sale by all booksellers, or will be sent by the publishers,
postage prepaid, on receipt of price.*

ILLUSTRATIONS

A FAMILY CANOE TRIP

I

GERNEGROSS lay at the foot of the dock steps; tins, tent, rubber beds, blankets —the whole camping outfit of three people for six weeks—under her bright decks and in the twelve canvas bags hung by genius around her tiny cockpit.

The Captain descended to the rear seat, and jointed his paddle. His wife sat down in the middle, and jointed hers. Their little boy scrambled to the front and gathered up the steering-lines.

" But you have not told us your route yet," complained one on the dock.

The three smiled up into the faces bent over the cockle-shell of a boat in envy, amusement, contempt, anxiety. And the Captain answered, " My dear people, except for the canoe meet on Willsborough Point

at the full of the August moon, we haven't
any plans."

The paddles slanted. "Good - bye!'
"God by 'e!"

We were out in the current. Behind us
arose voices, as of the life we were leaving
But the north wind sweeping the great river
cried louder in our ears of the life beginning
as we passed beyond sight of the waving
handkerchiefs, and came up with the bridge
boat *Susie*, moored to a pier underneath the
mammoth bridge.

The pilot looked out of his window.

"Well, sir, there's no telling when the
tow 'll be up, with this wind against it.
Hadn't you better come aboard?"

And aboard—fit beginning of a journey
without plan—we spent the afternoon. The
flame of an iron-furnace reddened on the
changing sky, the last sunshine made a
light-and-shade mosaic upon the western
hills, and chapel bells were knolling to
prayer, when a cry rose up, "The tow!"

Huge, shadowy, it came crawling on in
the dusk, a line of forty canal-boats with
two tugs ahead. Away steamed the *Susie* to
meet it, drew up broadside with the last boat

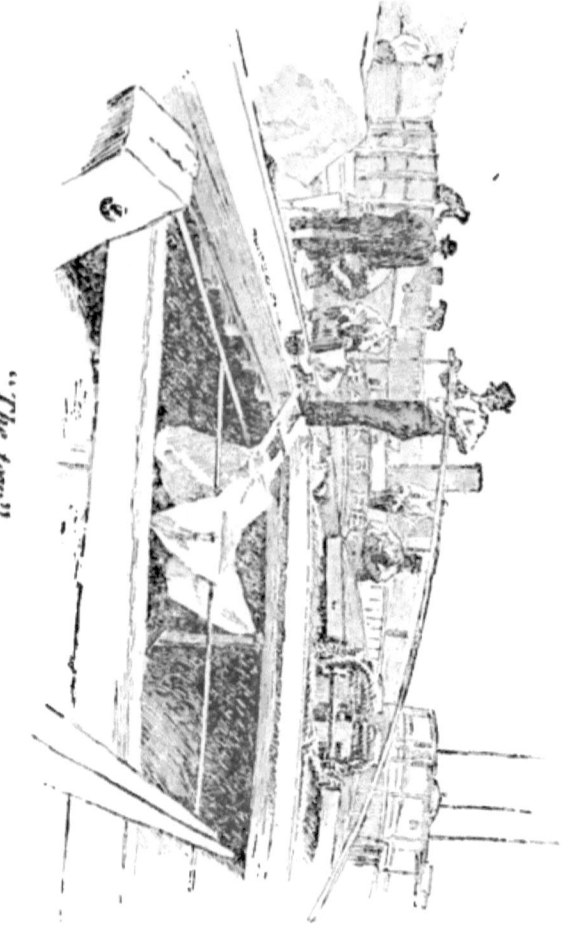

"The tow"

of the fleet, the *Delaphine-of-Windsor*, set us aboard, and made off with a friendly salute.

We peered into the shadows. Near us a thin woman stood with folded arms at the head of her cabin stairs. A dark girl stared from the next boat. Beyond were more faces, and a grotesque jumble of cabin roofs and poles and nameless things on the ungainly decks far out towards the snorting tugs. The city lights were slipping behind. Already we were part of another life—a life which, passing us year after year upon the summer river, was yet as unknown as life upon Ganges or Nile. And we were stirred by that sense of the new which makes the delight of childhood; aye, and of manhood, too; though men, in their little paddocks of pleasure or duty or thought, lament to Heaven that the days are dull.

"The party that's to go to Troy with us?" spoke up the thin woman, with a glimmer of a smile. "If you like, ma'am, I'll show you below."

She dipped under the cabin roof. As we saw in the lamplight her young face with its pale hair and eyes, we seemed to find her spirit, like her gown, faded but immaculate.

"Here's your room." And with a prim, delightful little air of doing all things "proper," she pushed open a door. The state-room might, indeed, be termed snug; but so tidy was it that, as we looked back into the cabin, and saw the range in a recess, and shelves of tins over it, and the covered table, and curtained windows, and plants growing, and pictures, and the clock, and the bird-cage, it appeared unreasonable, not to say absurd, that a man should ever ask for more than this; except, perhaps, upon a rare occasion—say, the Thanksgiving dinner of a large family.

We took seats in the cabin—all of us, including the captain of the *Delaphine-of-Windsor*, who came stepping to his place with a heedfulness in every muscle gratifying to see in a man. He was a well-built Yankee, with a shrewd, manly look, his embrowned face and tarnished black curls set off by a shirt of yellow with scarlet patches.

Looking from one to another of us, he said, in a musical drawl, "Goin' on the water for a vacation? Sacred Peter!"

"Where would you go?" asked *Gernegross's* captain.

"Why, on a picnic, in the woods—any place where a man could be *on the land!*"

After that, conversation flowed on as between persons mutually interesting.

The people? All steady Americans, 'cept them Canucks next door. That girl and her brother had been on the water all their lives, and now they were running the boat alone; and the father was a rich man on Lake Champlain.

Business good? Waal, not in *these* times. Easy life? Sometimes. Plague of it was, it was so easy part o' the time, a man hadn't strength for the tough work when it *did* come—the loadin' and unloadin' at the ends o' the trips.

"It must be pleasant, though," we thought, "and safe."

He smiled. "Waal, moderately. If a line don't slacken when a man's crossin' it. Or you don't happen to be the last boat. Of a dark night. In the city." Between each clause he stopped, and at the end he gathered his knee into his arms, and tipped back his chair.

"Six months ago. About three o' the mornin'. A tug run intew the last boat.

An old boat, it was. Sunk inside of tew minutes. The people? Waal, there was father and mother and tew children. Three o' them got clear. All 'cept the baby. Then the man dove. Ten foot plumb down. Never expected to see him again. He went raight intew the cabing—the ruff had come clean off—and grabbed the baby out o' the berth. First thing we see, up come the baby's head out o' the water."

When, late, we went upon deck and beheld the dazzle of the Milky Way, and, sprawling beneath it, the black company of boats marked off by tiny windows and drowsy deck lanterns, and near us *Gernegross*, with her cosey secrets covered up in canvas, over all there seemed brooding that spirit of mystery and of danger which quickens an adventure. Then an accordion sounded, and led rough young voices in a chorus—wild, defiant, plaintive. It came from the French girl's cabin, and through her window we saw her face under the meek face of the Virgin.

At five of the morning, mounting our stairs, we found the men and boys of the fleet splitting wood, and pumping with the aid of long elastic saplings, and at each cabin stove-pipe the smoky streamer of the lady getting breakfast below. The sky was streaked with faint cirrus clouds, and glowing eastward. On our right, the City of Hudson lay ramparted by sedges. On our left, the village of Athens—locally A-thens —showed embowered lanes. Still farther westward, the Catskills lifted their "slopes full of slumber."

The stir of breakfast over, we glided on like an enchanted caravan, lulled by a gurgling as of rushing brooks between the boats. The men, in groups, hugged their knees on the cabin roofs or lay on elbow along the decks. On the *Maria Dagwell* a stout woman sat with folded arms under a yellow umbrella. Beyond her, on the *Angeline Allore*, a baby ran upon the cabin roof, waving its arms, and threatening, the livelong hours, to tumble into the river. Still farther on, two children swung ceaselessly in a hammock. The French girl, after shrilly quarrelling with her tall brother, made quick work of her dishes, and took her place upon the cabin stairs. Our little boy went a-fishing, a rope tied around his waist. His father roused some excitement by swinging, camera on back, from boat to boat. Our hostess did her washing, with her model husband working the machine and putting up poles and lines. Presently he came to smile at the picketed little boy.

" But do the children never fall in ?" We pointed to the lurching baby.

He laughed. " No; they get used to it."

As we drew near Albany, noisy little tugs, mounting each a gilt eagle or a cock, began to surround the fleet. Their captains, the gentry of boatmen, better dressed and lordlier than the canallers, came on board, and there was a mighty haggling over the price of a tow to Troy. The *Delaphine-of-Windsor's* bargain made, her tug travelled beside us, its engineer advising *Gernegross's* captain concerning the best methods of obtaining power from steam, and its handsome young pilot apparently lost in some " Dream of Fair Women " as he stood with his hand on the wheel and his eyes on the horizon.

Then, in the late afternoon, in a gathering mist, arose gray before us the spires and domes of Albany. What is there in this

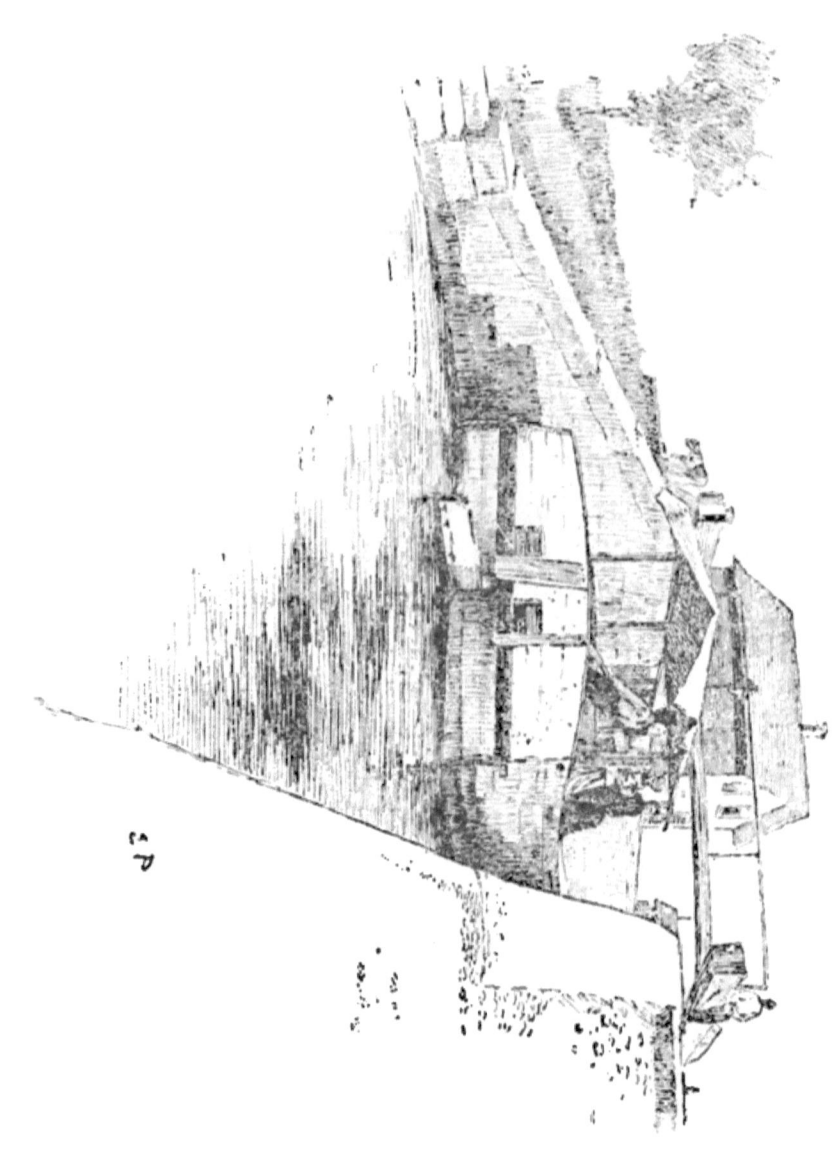

first glimpse of a dim city, be it New York, Antwerp, or Rome, to move one? Why, at the sight, is the heart fit to break? What instinct says, " At last?" Is the vision, may-hap, prototype of a heavenly vision, at sight of which, some day, we shall cry, " Home?"

But what has happened to our enchanted caravan? Here are shouts, calls; men run-ning, ropes flinging; boats parting, swinging out in great curves; tugs, puffing in between them, making fast their convoys. We, alone, are drifting backward down the river.

" What's this mean?" cries the captain of the *Delaphine-of-Windsor* to the dreamful pilot.

" Now don't be excited, cap'n. I'll have you there as soon as the best of 'em. You've no cause to go and get mad."

The captain smokes, and is sulky. Perch-ed along the cabin roof, we await the result.

Veritably, we are passing all our friends! The French girl stares after us, the stout lady turns to look, the baby screams, the girls in the hammock sit up—we are by, we are under the bridge, only one boat ahead of us! But to her a second tug makes fast.

" Let her run!" cries our pilot. " That

On the Towpath

thing couldn't pull a settin' hen off her
nest !''

On we forge in the rain, past Albany, between dim shores. Inch by inch we gain on
our rival. Who suspects the rapture of a
canal-boat race? Our brave little tug pants,
throbs—with a toot, a shout, we are by, and
swing, first, into the lock at West Troy !

We look across to lighted Troy, rising
mysteriously in the darkness, while our boat-
man's wife confides to us that she is glad to
be out of the river, where she never feels
safe, and to be going home. Then something gives way before us, and we pass out;
and lie moored until a driver is engaged and
clearance papers are secured from the col-
lector's office, to the "master for this present
passage" of the "boat, canoe *Gernegross*."

And now we begin to move slowly up the
canal. Plainly, here is no chance for camping. We go below. But all through the
night we are conscious of the plodding
mules; of the bargee at the heavy tiller,
throwing his whole weight upon it at some
curve; of a shout at intervals, "Ye-ho, lock !"
and the faint answer from the lockman ahead,
" Aye, aye !"

II

Most people think a canal is a line of black ooze, which crawls at the rear of factories and past the door-yards of scurvy cabins, their refuse on its banks, and their reek in its water.

But he who wanders with it knows that a canal is a stream curving to the heart of meadow and wood; that the towpath is a grassy fringe; the heel-path a tangle of clematis, asters, golden-rod; that the white bridges and the clouds and the trees above him look up again from beneath him, so that he floats between; that weirs make falling music; that now he is borne across a brook, now high over the current of a river.

Early in the morning our friends of the *Delaphine-of-Windsor* lowered *Gernegross* as though she were an egg-shell, and helped down her people. They said little; but their eyes questioned her to the next bend.

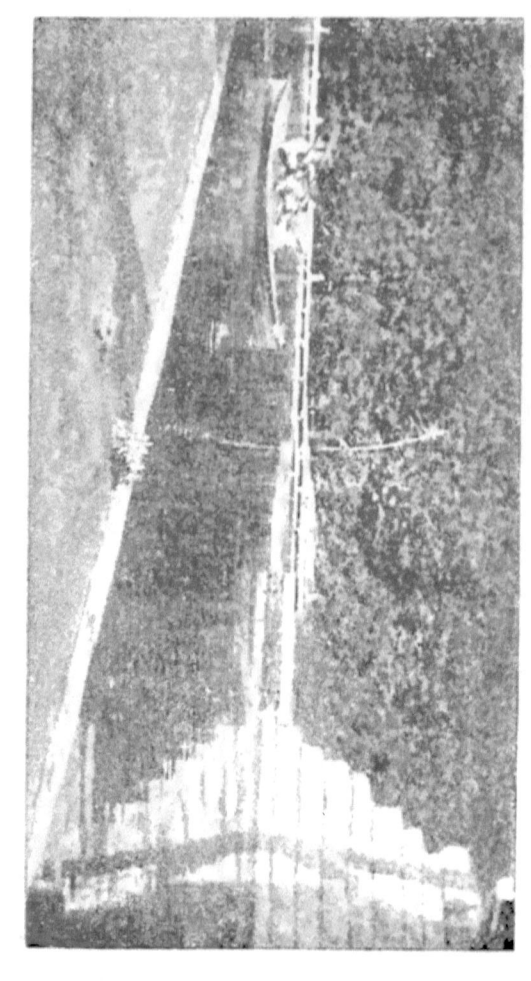

"*The white bridges . . . look up again from beneath*"

So the children of the Old World, it may be,
eyed Ulysses's vanishing craft.

After the rain the land sparkled—happy
farms upon the plain, overwatched by a line
of northward-southward trending hills, and
by towering cloud cumuli. " We of the sky
send greeting," meadow-larks piped down.
" Hurrah!" the little boy shouted back.
Then he sang to our paddling, " Isn't it jolly
to be all alone?" We thought it was—alone
with life and love, and naught superfluous.
We, best, knew it to be rare. Had we not
at home drawn bolts upon the world, and
still found it before us at the hearth, bab-
bling?

Mowers stopped their whirring machines
to gaze after us. Now we passed a house;
a smiling woman ran out, and, with a pro-
priety that savored of genius, waved a tea-
pot in honor of domesticity afloat. Suddenly a meditative party of mules and a man
appeared upon the towpath, for harbingers;
then a clumsy round prow, as of a Spanish
galleon, loomed around a curve and came on
—slow, inevitable. The family aboard ran
together to stare at us. Our camera stood
ready; and we fixed it all—mules, boat, and

people—against an exquisite curve of the bank.

"Hi! look at the toy boat!" cried a girl, running with a baby from a group of cottages. More children followed her; and the train, trotting beside us, brought us with distinction to our first lock.

The lock store stood at one side. Tins, pails, brooms, yellow oilers dangling like defunct seamen, ornamented the porch; and upon a slab set up like a tombstone was this inscription: "Tea, coffee, sugar, spices, flour, crackers, lard, pork, fish, starch, cheese, kerosene, tobacco, boots and shoes, MILK." Dominic Dumas had his name writ above the door. He proved to be a genial old Irishman, befogged, at sight of us, with wonder.

"Ain't ye 'feared ye'll drown thim young wans?" he called down from the lever. "Och, aye, I'll let ye up aisy!"

The black gates swung open with a silent invitation. We entered. They closed behind us. Blocks of green, polished, slimy stone rose ten feet on either side. A boy caught the rope we threw, and passed it around a post chafed by many ropes into

"Loomed around a curve, and came on—slow, inevitable"

the semblance of a South American idol.
The cataract pouring over the upper gates
slackened. And, with a roar, a dozen
streams came forcing up from below in
whirlpools that boiled over against each
other, and spread back, and caught at *Gerne-gross*, and rocked and swung her, and strained her rope, and filled the place with foam,
and flung up spray, and shouted riotously.
But the stanch little thing rose steadily until she lay at the coping-stone, and bore us
out into a land that, after that tumult, looked
more than ever like a happy vision. While
Dominic Dumas called after us :

"Where ye goin'? Glens Falls? Ye'll be
whiles gettin' there, thin!"

Paddling on, we thought of weariness ;
then forgot it, and, an hour after, found
ourselves fresh again. That is the advantage of paddling. There is no strain. The
muscles soon play of themselves to the
rhythm. Each day there is less effort in the
lazy motion, until one fancies one might fall
asleep, and still keep paddling on.

At the next lock, in the joy of our hearts,
we delivered over our purse to the little boy.
The store being thus open to him, he and

the obsequious lock-man brought out a treasure of bananas, peanuts, gumdrops, and root-beer. Which delicacies supplementing our locker, we nooned upon a sightly knoll.

That afternoon we varied paddling with towing. It allowed of more intercourse with the people we met; and of the traveller's play. "Can you tell us the name of those hills?" we would ask. "Dunno'," would be the usual answer. But one canal-man told us, "You won't think much o' them little things when you see the big ones up yander." And a young farmer "ruther guessed they were some belongin's of the Green Mountings."

We became acquainted with our fellow-travellers, the mule-drivers — "Father Tom," and "Long Level," and "Teddy Timber-Toe," and "Spavined Tim"—men crippled, maimed, the very drift and wreckage of society. In face they were less moral than the mules they drove: now a sallow Yankee with a hint of lost estate in his unquiet eyes; now an all-brutal, shaggy foreigner. "They are a rough lot," a canalman had told us, "but they'll not harm you." We found them civil, even obliging.

But they whacked their beasts viciously, vituperated one another in passing, and were blots upon the idyllic land.

It was still early afternoon, while we were skirting a wood, that a quiet basin opened to us. Around it the trees rose tier on tier, and along their tops ran a whisper of invitation. *Gernegross* heard. Dragon - flies guided her to a dam and a water-fall and a ruined mill-wheel.

And now, with the explorer's ardor upon us, we ran about to find a clearing and the two trees for the tent. Quickly it was pitched, and, before the door, the table set with each man's complement of tins. Then, in a hollow lined with leaves, dry wood was heaped, and stakes set up, and our kettle swung on its chain, and an incense of cocoa and broiling ham sent up to the fauns and dryads.

"The flapjack," proclaimed our captain then, "is the appropriate beginning of camp cookery. And I am he who can flap it !"

Fine to hear was the little boy's shriek as each cake fell over in the pan. But let no epicure dream that a recipe can impart the

secret of that flavor.   For it the gypsy fire
is needed—and the canoist's appetite.

As to how we rested : we had meant to
lie and listen to the night sounds, to peep
out and see the stars wheel, and surprise the
trees at their gossip.   But, inadvertently,
we closed our eyes—and the tent was yellow with morning light.

As we went on up the canal the hills
dropped behind us.   Then, one noon, the
first peak of the Adirondacks appeared at
the north, and summoned his brothers, and
they rose along the horizon, and by sunset
stood guarding their solitudes.   They had
no friendly welcome for us.   They sent a
storm which chased away our golden weather.   The land lay deserted, and we had it
with the wet cows, and the birds calling
back and forth.   Why do people dislike to
be out in the rain ?   The air is at its freshest ;
the senses are lulled by the monotony of
sweet sounds and of quiet tints.   The doc-
tors should prescribe a rain cure for American nerves, where the patients shall sit apart
in flannels and mackintoshes and listen to
the rain.

Next, the Glens Falls' feeder gave us its

thirteen successive locks to climb, while the land fell a hundred and fifty feet behind us. And then a strong tide detained us, and kept us swinging around curves a full hour after we had descried the roofs and spires of Glens Falls against the cloudy mountains.

But when *Gernegross* had been borne in a triumphal procession to the hotel stable, and we had gone that evening to watch the work of the huge illuminated lumber-mill, from its hoisting the log out of the black water to its devil's dance of the saws over the white plank, it was then that we caught, at last, a whisper—a message—the voice of the Adirondacks :

"If storm, if toil, if weariness cannot daunt you, we count you worthy. Come up to the hills !"

III

WE left Glens Falls in state—*Gernegross* billowed upon a cart, and her crew bestowed in a phaeton—and went clumping along a fine plank-road into "the dark and dangerous pass to Lake George."

Instead of Indians, there were tots of farmers' children offering us peaches and apples; one perched upon a horse-post, one reading demurely behind a tiny table—choice pictures for our camera. And now the hills, their purple doffed, rose to west and north in rugged undress. "You have come!" they said to us. "Receive of our exultant life." The pines mounted crag on crag in the sunshine. Over the valley falling eastward circled an eagle. Crows cawed. Little birds in thicket twittered, "Tee-wee, tee-wee, wee-wee-wee."

A light upon the plain— a sheet of blue— "The lake!" Rattling down into the village

"*Instead of Indians*"

of Caldwell, we circled the Indian encamp-
ment—where the little boy sold his heart to
dark maidens for bows and arrows and
mimic canoes—passed a street of hotels, and
came out upon the shore.

Spirits of the brave! Had they gone up
in slaughter but to return to earth again, as
Orient teaches? and did we see them in that
gala armament, in those maidens in blouses,
those trig youths, those children and nurses
and loiterers to hotel music?

"Then how are the mighty fallen!"
thought that little savage, *Gernegross*, with
an ache in her side for the cool plunge. A
workman dropped his can, a gentleman with
a noble gray head came from his launch,
and both helped her in.

"You will find canoists all the way," said
the gentleman. "They are drawing to their
Meet, you know. Diamond Island," he
pointed northward, "is your nearest and
best camp." And he and his ladies waved
us *bon voyage*.

The hotels, the little boats, the villas of
nook and knoll, were left behind. Sunset
came. Azure and golden and crimson lights
of the sky, pink and pale purple shapes of

the horizon, near mountains, islands — all were mirrored in the pure and tranquil water. And sound of convent bells—*real* convent bells—came to us on breaths of cedar and pine. This was Father Jogues's " Holy Lake;" and we floated on, ravished by its beauty.

" Here we are! Let me out! Hurrah!" shouted the little boy, capering along the rocks like the " Last of the Mohicans" himself.

" Father, here's a landing, a really, truly one ! And, mother, I've found a camp already—all pine prickers, *so* deep !"

Happy sight of a child's joy in the " sufficing face of nature !" Nor shall the one over whom it broods like face of mother be lightly taken by the vulgar or evil lures of life. So we landed ; and presently supped, with a white tent across on the main-land for company. And early asleep, alas ! still caught, in dreams, snatches of the songs of passing rowers.

When we awoke, two small cedars were decorating our walls with dancing shadows. Then said our captain, " To-day we sail !" Contrary to all traditions of camping, on

" The lake "

that morning we slighted breakfast, and stowed our duffle hastily. While yet it was early, we cut our sapling mast, set our square sail like a Norse galley's, and to the chorus, "For it's up with the bonnets of bonny Dundee," shot from Diamond Island.

For the honor of the thing, we put out trolling lines. But who could mope for fish with that ripple along the keel, and that soughing in the ear? Instead, our sailing grew to a quest for the most beautiful island. In the afternoon we found it, and camped upon it. And there, in the idyllic days that followed — it is the secret of our trip — we built our summer cottage. We put the playground at one end, where the blissful children might play in freedom among the rocks ; at the other, upon an inaccessible crag, the study. For the rest, it combines the beauty of each cottage on the lake with others all its own. You shall surely know it by this token—never is a headache nor a heartache there.

At —— we heard of Mr. Windham.

"Camp at High Point to-night," a hotel-keeper told us. " My brother is in charge of a cottage there, and he's always glad to make it handy for campers."

A kindred spirit! We took to the paddles, and at dusk drew near to a cape that was sombre with darkling pines. On a rock, his hands in his pockets, stood a thin, smiling man.

"That's it! Right in here," he called. "Felt it in my bones there'd be campers here to-night! That pavilion there, sir, is a tent, floored to your hand. And up at the cottage, ma'am, I've a fire at your service."

Seated in a rocking-chair at the cottage, he cheerily explained to us how he "usually kept things pretty well picked up; but last night he thought the dishes might as well lie till mornin'. And then this mornin' he sort o' took a notion to go fishin'"—surely it explained itself. Mr. Windham clearly was a bit of a genius, with gentle interests peopling the solitudes of his life. He was full of stories and legends of the lake; of Roger's slide and the Mohican maiden, and the French and Indian battles; of Hunt, the hermit artist; and of ——, the romantic hotel-keeper of Black Mountain.

"I've lived in these parts twenty years,"

"Mirrored in the pure and tranquil water"

he said, "and it don't look a bit the worse.
No, I've never been to New York. I suppose a man might be there weeks and not
see it all. One thing I would like to see,
though, and that's the World's Fair at Chee-
cawgo. But I don't suppose I'll get to it."

Neither did we suppose so, when, a few
mornings later, we left him on his shore.
We thought he would continue rocking in
his chair, and "sort o' takin' notions to go
fishin'" instead of washing up the dishes;
with longings stirring him only pleasantly
the while to "see things."

That was a sublime dark day, meet for the
sailing of the Narrows. With the clouds
dragging the sides of the mountains, and a
gale driving us swiftly on, the strait might
have been a wild Northern fiord. We ran
in at Hague for supplies, nooned upon an
island, and afterwards crossed the lake, and
went hugging the eastern cliffs as only canoists can, gathering red and orange lich-
ens, and ferns and harebells from the ledges.
Presently we heard the ring of an axe, and,
rounding a point, came upon an old blackened farm-house in a lonesome spot at the
foot of a mountain; and upon the axeman,

who looked uncomfortably like a bandit,
until he smiled and said :

"Camp?   Right here, sir, or anywhere
about, just as you like. Cut down whatever
you want."

The sky threatening now, we hurried the
tent up, and had everything under cover by
the time the rain began.   Then, inside, we
lighted our small alcohol stove, and opened
a can of clam chowder, and supper was
steaming when we heard voices. Lifting our
tent flap, we saw, out in the twilight, two
barelegged sturdy little fellows from the
farm-house, rain-drops falling from their
torn hat-brims.

We fell to converse with them.   School?
Just over that mounting. They liked it best
in winter, 'cause more boys went then, and
it was more fun ; and then they took sleds
and slid down, one way goin' and another
way comin'.   Fish ?   Lots just around there.
Jim Stone, up to Ti, knew all the places.
Worms ?   Yes, sir ; they'd dig 'em, and have
'em ready in the mornin'.   Good-night !

The rain had ceased. The woods were
still. Looking out for a last picture of water
and mountain and sky, we beheld, over *Ger-*

"A sheet of blue"

negross in her cove, a token—the boat of heaven, the new moon, her prow lifted to ride the skyey waves. Our time was up on the " Lake of the Blessed Sacrament."

IV

LAKE GEORGE grows less clear as it begins to flow into Ticonderoga Creek—first
a reedy stream, then five leaps to great
Champlain. Paper-mills hide the falls.
Down the descending curve straggles Ticonderoga village.

An inhabitant, whose business was to
"dicker in wegetables," navigated *Gerne-*
gross down the dusty main street. Was it
only the mid-day heat that dulled the eyes
of women at windows, and of sitters on hotel
steps? Even at those life centres, the grocery store and the post-office, the pulse of
" Ti " beat low. World-weariness was upon
her, and upon us when we came again to
the creek.

Once the water there floated war-vessels,
the "dickerer in wegetables" said. Now it
was very shallow. But *Gernegross* slipped
in, never so glad and never so pretty. Lily-

pads netted across her way. We wound our arms down the long stems, drew them up, and with lilies heaped and crowned her. The water deepened. The air freshened. The afternoon mellowed with opalescent lights. And earth was once again "the garden of the Lord" when we entered "the Lake that is the Gate of the Country."

"Here we are! These are the heights of Carillon. The French named them from the chiming water-falls, you remember. And that ruin above, my boy, that—"

"Oh, father, I know! Fort—Fort—"

"But you'll tip the boat over!"

"Oh, mother, don't tell me! It's Ti—Ti —*Titangeroga!* Hurrah!"

At a strip of beach below the fort lay a boat of deep-sea blue. Floating by and slowly skirting Carillon, we looked up. Watching us from a crag was a gentleman in gray boating suit and cap; behind him a tent flying the Stars and Stripes.

We rested on our paddles.

"Any place for a camp up there?"

The gentleman descended — lithe, sunburnt, with a smile beaming from one blue eye and whimsical wrinkles closing the

other, as though the sun were too much for
both at once.

"Yes, sir ; very good. We have found a
pleasant spot up under those trees, as you
see. And beyond us, under the two oaks,
is another."

"I believe I will go up."

The two scrambled away together. A
moment, and down the rocks came, "All
right!"

The gentleman—Professor H——, of ——
College—had camped many summers on
Lakes George and Champlain, and in the
Adirondacks. Camping last year, he had
met his wife. And now they were upon their
wedding-tour. "Visiting our old haunts,"
he said, with a gesture around, and that
charming, one-eyed smile. Up at his tent
there was a look of old campers—a rustic
table with tins, camp-chairs, and, last luxury
of camp life, a stove-top set upon stones,
with a length of pipe pouring forth smoke
and sparks.

"Just make free with our fire," said the
Professor.

Then, with great kindness and agility, he
helped tote up our luggage. As coffee

steamed and steak broiled, we advanced in
acquaintance — ladies, by way of the weather and the view; gentlemen, by the absorbing, vital way of boats, tents, fishing.
And when our own little house was ready,
and we were supping before it, dreamily we
smiled upon each other,

"Oh, rest ye, brother mariners, we will not wander more."

The next day was the phenomenal hot day
of the summer. Even on the heights of
Carillon it was hot. The morning began
with a calamity. As our breakfast pot was
sweet to the nostrils, the little boy, sniffing,
begged to stir. Alas! no rock-balanced pot
could out-sit that childish energy. A stir too
hard—and our breakfast was hurrying fifty
feet sheer down, the little boy crying out,
we staring hungrily after it. Eating in camp
is not the flimsy matter it is at home. The
whole day hangs upon the three pegs of
breakfast, dinner, and supper.

The heat told upon the company. Only
the good Professor went and came upon his
errands, an ideal camper, bringing in a load
of brushwood as though stepping to ecstatic
music. The little boy, in airy costume of

trunks and life-preserver, went swimming.
Then the Professor, in duck suit and over-
shoes, came down to wash his boat. Then
the Captain came down with an Adirondack
map, and the two men sat planning trips,
while little snipe—"tip-ups" the Professor
called them—ran along the sand. A king-
fisher flapped near; a herd of cows descended the hills, and stood udder-deep in
the lake.

But towards evening the wind that lives at
Carillon awoke, and thenceforth never failed
us. Energy revived. A walk to the fort
was planned.

As we entered the Professor's camp a
stranger sat there—a bronzed, cadaverous
man, with wrinkles like ruts, and glassy
black eyes. He wore a checked yellow suit,
a green necktie, a wide slouched hat, and
carried a gray cotton umbrella tied with
twine.

"Yes, sir, it lays right there!" he was saying. "Ain't more'n six feet of water over
it. A brass six-inch cannon!"

"Dear me!" cried the Professor, rubbing
his hands. "I'd like to get it out, first-rate!
first-rate! We'll locate it. My friend Gen-

" Oh, rest ye, brother mariners "

eral W—— will go in for it I'm sure. And
we'll hire a diver, and have it out!"

"Around in the crick," continued the stranger, "lays a ship sunk. A pay ship. Mill-
ions aboard. She was almost took. And
the British cap'n, he scuttled her. There's
a man in New York sends a gang of men up
every summer to dig for her. He's sunk
$25,000 a'ready. But that brass cannon"—
he contemptuously turned his back upon
the gentlemen —"that I've seen myself."
He threw a tantalizing glance back over his
shoulder. "Water ain't more'n six foot
over it!"

Then, gallantly, he addressed himself to
the ladies. "Plenty of sceneries around
here," with a sweep of the umbrella. "Up
there"—he took aim at Mount Independ-
ence—"is one scenery."

"How I should like to climb it!" said the
Professor's wife. "But are you sure there
are no snakes there?"

"*Snakes!*" The eyes of the stranger
emitted yellow gleams. "It's full—chock-
full—of rattlesnakes!"

"Oh!" cried the Professor's wife.

"And this time of year, in the dog-days.

they're *blind*. And when they're blind,
they're fierce, ma'am, fierce! Then there's
adders; and there's mountain-racers. They
chase a man. Run as fast as he can. Only
way to 'scape 'em is to dodge 'em. They
just whip around a man's middle, snap into
a bow-knot, and squ-ee-ze him dead!"

No eye of ancient mariner ever glittered
more. The grewsome stranger plucked a
handful of grass and chewed at it with an
unnatural relish, as though it were his common diet.

"There's a man I know—Tim Toby. Last
winter he was sot to blast out foundation-
stone for the new mill up to Ti. Clearin'
out rubbish from the foot of the ledge, he
dropped in dynamite catridges. And, sir,
she blew out—snakes! A great heap; all
kinds; 278 of 'em. Hed crawled in to
winter. Well, sir, Tim lit out for Ti. Never
stopped for his tools. As white "—the stranger looked down over his paper collar—"as
my shirt. And sezee to the owners, 'I took
that contract to get out foundation-*stone*. I
didn't calklate you wanted to build your
mill of snakes!'"

"My dear, you are pale." said the Professor, rousing from his dream of finding the cannon. "The heat has been too much for you. Come, to the fort! I suppose, sir"— as we all started up the hill—"relics are still dug here?"

"Hev been. But now it's agin the law. Except you be a redskin. They can dig and chop down anywhere."

"Do you mean to say the Indians can come and dig in our gardens at home?"

"Anywhere in the hull land, ma'am. Put down so in the treaty. And any court in the land 'll uphold 'em in it!"

We wound around under the grassy ramparts hung with tangle of hawthorn and wild-grape. We stopped to look into the choked well. Then, as we gained the summit of the breastworks, our eyes went from the little plain at our feet, once bustling with military life, out over the great lake, to the ridges of those Green Mountains whence came the immortal "Boys."

"They stole across that locust-covered flat," explained our Professor. "They came climbing this little winding way. Down there must be where the sentinel snapped his musket at Ethan Allen, missing fire,

And here—yes, here must be where he made his entrance into the commandant's chamber; and when asked in whose name he demanded surrender, cried, ' In the name of the Great Jehova hand the Continental Congress !' "

We scattered about the parade-ground, where the wind was in the thistle and the velvet mullein ; then went defiling through a roofless passage.

" Here was their oven." The stranger pointed to a blackened spot. " Where they put in a hull beef. Good cement they made in them days," knocking down a bit with his umbrella. " French brick, you see. Ah, the France French are a fine nation, whether for settin' the styles, or for buildin' houses ; the only really ingenious nation on the face of the earth. I'm three - quarters France French myself."

Through a window, whose sill was yellow with buttercups, we could see little gabled houses in Ti sending up tinted smoke; a charmed, tender picture, framed by ruin and decay.

But the rest had gone crawling along a way half filled with new-fallen rubbish. We found them sitting, thoughtful, around a hole.

"It is a shame the country lets it crumble," the Captain was saying. "A few more years, frosts, storms, and the site — perhaps the very name—will be forgotten."

"And yet the part it played!" said the Professor. "That surrender did more than any one thing to hearten the country, as she began her struggle. It took away the fear of invasion by way of Canada, and it pinned the people's faith to that little council called the 'Continental Congress.' Yes, there was genius in that cry of Ethan Allen's. But— though it isn't told in history—he died a pauper, and his grave is unknown."

When we came back to the little white tents on the cliff, we were in quiet mood.

But the wind was not.

"Do you suppose the tents will stand it?" our Captain called down the hill the last thing that night.

A dim figure, upon its knees in the camp below, answered, "Oh yes; I am only tightening my lanyards. Good-night."

Ghosts of that long struggle for the "Lake that is the Gate of the Country," were they

At the Fort

all abroad, shrieking their old cries? Hu-
rons; Algonquins, Five Nations, their fury?
Soldiers—French, English, American—their
agony, defeat, triumph? Now singly; now
joining, swelling, to one awful cry—must not
the sky crash, pass, let in the great Revela-
tion? A lull, and the crickets, and the creaking pendulum of a tree-toad—

And a voice, " The tent is down !"

We sat erect.

" The pole hit me square on the head."
But the laugh was reassuring.

We thought. The wind howled.

" What time is it ?"

" Three o'clock."

There came a gust that bellied the folds
about us.

" I believe," hesitated the Captain, " we
might—almost—leave her as she is—for the
rest of the night."

" Do!" For it was drear to think of
struggling, deserted of Heaven, with the
poles and the wind on the brink of the cliff.
" There is air enough, and room enough ;
and not half as much noise as there was
before. If only "—looking down on a small
bundle—" *he* won't be frightened."

"What's the matter?" said a sleepy little voice. And then, "Ho, ho! isn't it jolly!"

So our tent arose when the sun did.

Later, the Professor came with his oars over one shoulder and his stove-pipe over the other, to start a search for relics.

"But why the stove-pipe?"

With dignity and solemnity he answered: "Through a pipe put down in the water, one can see the bottom. We're going to locate that brass cannon."

V.

THE brass cannon was never located. Even the good Professor began to fear that the stranger might be " one of those unfortunate beings who have an abnormal natal tendency, strongly developed by circumstances, to misrepresent the truth."

Meanwhile, in heaven widened the August moon.

So that one morning, when the winds were favoring, *Gernegross* received her quota and spread her sail ; while the Professor and his wife ran up the hill and along the cliff, and from the topmost parapet of Carillon waved us salutes up the lake.

Great, empty, silent lake! In the days before railroads it used to be alive with dockyards, sailors, ships. Now, as we went speeding northward, we saw but one other sail—that of the lazy ferry-scow laden with meditative cows. The Adirondacks, phantasm of misty heights and passes, went with us on the west. On the east, the substantial but unused stone warehouses of shipping times gave to the shore that last lonesomeness—of the abandoned track of man. The passion and stir of life were left to the pale green waters with their rhythmic sw-is-sh, and to the writhing vapors overhead.

Had we lived in another age, we had felt sure, that afternoon, that the gods were pursuing us. For when the clouds had threatened long, suddenly an ink-black circle overhung us, mingled all shapes in sulphurous light, and fell in gray, pitiless downpour. But we only took to mackintoshes.

Whereupon, again the circle formed. We crept forward to unship our mast. With a roar, a gale lashed up the lake and rushed on *Gernegross*. But she lifted her saucy bow, rode the big waves, and danced atop; while the little boy laughed: "The water maidens are kissing me!"

So we triumphed. And the gods owned it; and shut up the wind; and smoothed the lake till it lay like burnished steel; and hung red banners in the sky; and brought us, weary mariners, to a sunset land, where

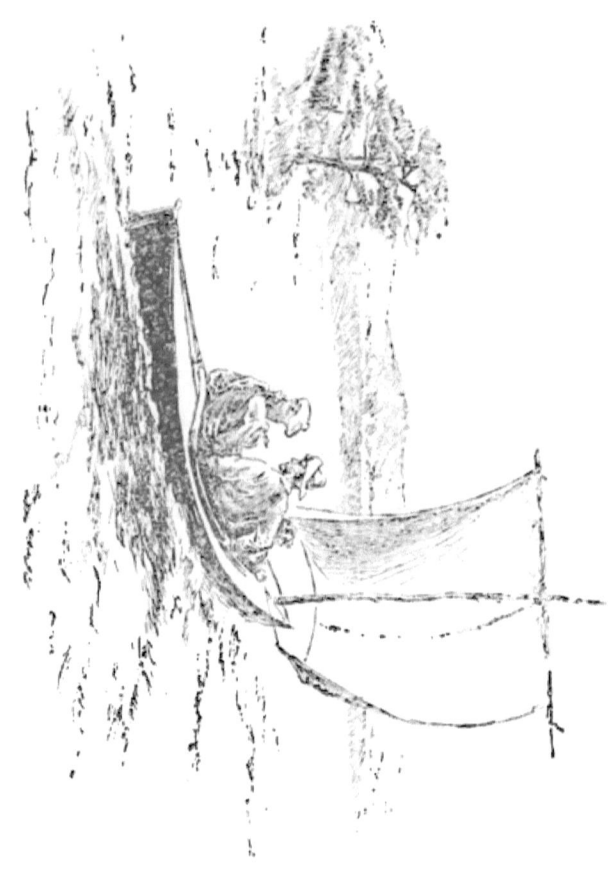

"'Gernegross'... spread her sail"

rose a pavilion with the flag of the A. C. A.
(which is American Canoe Association); and
sent, hastening to the little dock, a party
of solemnly eager children and their father.

"We have been watching all day for canoes. I am a member of the association,
though not much of a canoist myself. We
spend our summers here in the pines, and I
have joined for the pleasure of raising the
flag and decoying canoists ashore. To-
night, sir, you could not find a better camp
than beside us in the grove."

We were too tired for camping, we decided. But if there were a farm-house
near—

"There is one just beyond. We will
show you the way."

The children ran on before us, and out
into fields rising with soft slopes back to
the mountain wall.

"The finest iron-mines in the country are
only nine miles over the mountains," Mr
Thorp said. "If you are interested in such
things, why not stay and visit them?"

Why not, indeed? The trip had been
planned by the time we reached the farm-
house.

"A cabin. It was very gray and low"

This had the mark of aristocracy in the region—a square cupola, as of a New England meeting-house. Its one roof, extending over many out-buildings, gave the summer traveller a shivering reminder of the relentless winter, never far distant ; and the sweet - faced people who received us spoke and moved as though accustomed to the perpetual silence and solitude of snow. The heirlooms of ancestors who had wrestled for these fields, the clock and the creaking cupboard brought from Scotland, made more noise than they did.

After supper the Captain stirred things up by what should have been a flash-light picture, but was only an explosion. And then the grandmother laid her spectacles in the family Bible and told us this tale. It has so pointed a moral that we recommend it for a collection of *Tales of the Young*.

"My two uncles," said the little grandmother, " were the first men that ever built steamboats on the lake. They built two. They put all they had into 'em. The one's name was the *Phœnix*. She burned clear down to the water's edge. The other was the *Enterprise*. She sank."

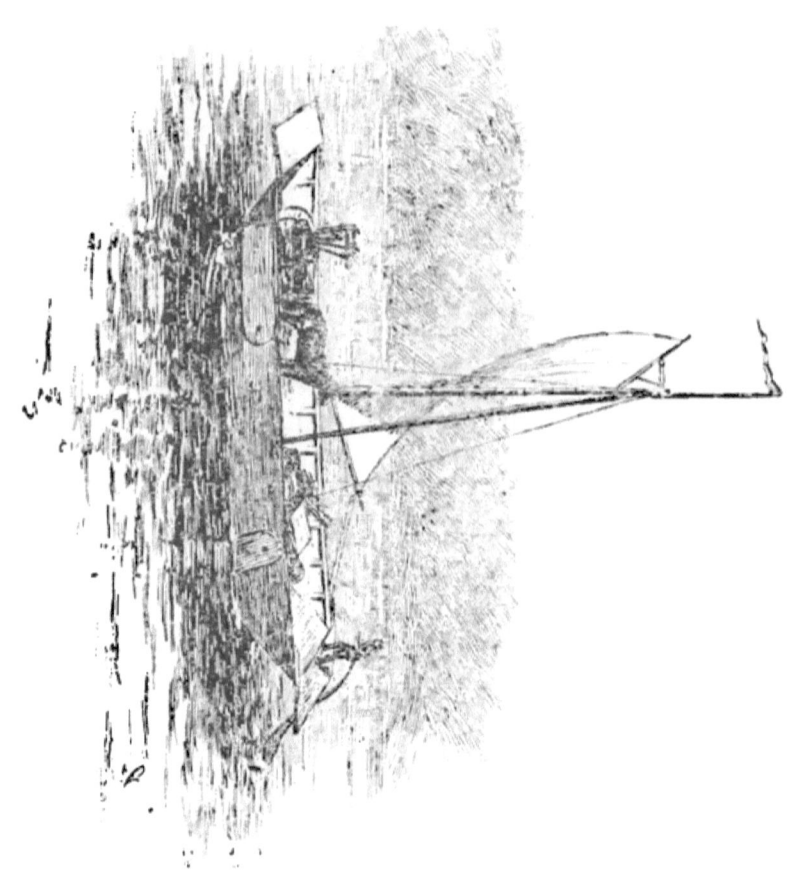

Yet we slept well upon it. The little boy even admitted: "It is nicer to sleep in a farm-house, though it is more fun in a tent." And the Captain dreamed of a canoe all of aluminum; so light that, only start her, and she would go forever!

Next morning, Mrs. Alexander, from her kitchen door, directed us across lots.

"You see that dash of sand—past that jag—around that clearing? That's the gap."

And we hastened over the fields. For this is a thing we delight in—to fling the reins to Fate, and let her gallop with us whither she will.

Leaving the clay of a former lake-bottom, we struck into the sand of a former lake-shore, and climbed steadily up among pines, beeches, poplars, and whitest of white birches. Often we turned to note the sinking of plain and lake; so that we were presently overtaken by a cart. The driver, a red-faced young fellow, whose trousers were a variegated landscape of clever patches, looked expressionless as a tree until his slow eyes found the little boy. Then they lighted, and he said, "Wouldn't the little chap like to ride?"

In the halt at every "thank you, ma'am," we learned about the few dwellings we passed, and about the mountains' other inhabitants. Foxes were many, and deer. Only the other day a doe had come into the garden to look for her fawn. And bears—small black ones. Every autumn they came to this deserted orchard for apples.

We drew up before a cabin. It was very gray and low. But the peaks overtopping it, and the sunflowers and hollyhocks pranking its walls, and the marigolds, phlox, four-o'clocks around it, made us think the good God liked to pour his own luxuries upon his mountaineers. A little white-haired child ran out, crying "Dad!"

The man lifted it, looked over its curls at us with a smile dawning from some depth, and said, "Won't ye come in to dinner?"

Wouldn't we? Not every day could we enter a kitchen-parlor like this one, with white bare floor, and window-shades with pictures, and masterpieces of mysterious dried bouquets upon the mantel. Not every day could we be served by such a dainty wild flower of a woman, nor see the Captain drink from a cup marked "A Good Child,"

nor find the little boy speechless a meal
through, his eyes upon a plate with Noah's
Ark in the middle, and all the animals out
in a procession on the rim.

They hung upon our words. They had
read about canoes and the Meet, but never
had seen a live canoist. They detained us
with pretexts. The little wife would show
us the house, halting in the guest-room that
we might mark the brand-new set of furni-
ture; and on the bureau—light of civiliza-
tion!—a red plush manicure-case. " It takes
some time to get things, when you hadn't
much to start with," she said, with, we were
glad to think, more of pride than apology.
And she ran merrily down with us to the
brook, where " John's mother used to wash,
and make fire under the big kettle. But
now John had made an aqueduct to the
house, and the washing isn't anything to
what it used to be."

In parting they asked, " Wouldn't we
please stop in on our way back?"

The afternoon walk was chiefly the de-
scent into Mineville.

Place of huge chimneys, of smoke, of
crazy plank walks, of miners' dwellings, of

At Mineville

saloons, of rushing machines, of a black, evil
pit in the centre, and white doves flutter-
ing up from it like souls out of purgatory.

Crouched in the buckets, we dropped 500
feet sheer down, and stepped out into an icy
chillness, among listless, blackened men. Cy-
clopean pillars rose above us in three tiers of
arches to the far sky; and beyond us sunk another pit, and down in it moved lights, which
meant, each, a man. Their shouts came hollow. There there were crashes, long rolls of
awful reverberations, and the stifling breath
of dynamite. It was joyful to rise again into
the sunlight; to be able to laugh at the little boy on a high stool proudly scrawling
his name in the visitors' book, and to give
thanks for the blessings of common day.

"Oh no! There was no place to eat or
sleep in Mineville," the grocery man said;
"but here was a wagon going five miles
up, and the driver Mr. McGill, the school-
master."

So, while crimson flakes filled the top of
the pass, and a whippoorwill sang, we listened
to the story of Barney McGill; how, a little
orphan boy, he had worked in the mines, and
studied betweentimes and nights, and saved

"A black evil pit"

enough to go away to school; how he had
come back to take the big Mineville school,
and quell and inspire its roughest spirits;
how, since, he had sent each sister away to
study and become a teacher. He told it as
modestly and bravely as he had lived it, and
then disappeared from our sight in a group
of laughing, pretty young women.

There was still a mile. The little boy en-
livened it by a discovery. "Ha! I see how
the stars come out: I was looking at a
spot, and a star popped out just like pop-
corn!" But we found it best not to stare
too long at any tree or bush, lest it should
take on form and motion "very like a bear."
And the small cabin, when we reached it,
rayed out upon the dark mountain-road a
cheery, welcome light.

We could see the mountaineer, in a fresh
shirt, reading aloud from his paper while his
wife sewed. A basin of the marigolds was on
the table. The shed door stood open. As we
walked in, both rose to meet us. He was un-
mistakably smiling now, and over his shoulder her voice came with an exultant ring:

"I told John you'd be back! Supper's
all ready."

VI

BACK again from the hills, we were all seated around a fire on Mr. Thorp's point —children laughing, sparks flying, stories going round—when the moon rose up, a full ellipse, and said, " Willsborough Point to-morrow !"

If the moon meant it, the lake did not. Next day there was a riot of sun, wind, and wave.   Along the rocky bastions of the shore the waters shouted in derision at sight of *Gernegross* as she labored around to meet each crest, and hurried down each trough.   But when the *Vermont* landed her Adirondack pilgrims at Westport that afternoon, *Gernegross* lay waiting on the dock, and was borne aboard.

Had Champlain broken its barriers? we wondered, when we steamed out from the beautiful town and bay : for, widening between the shadow-line of the Green Mount-

On Deck of the "Vermont"

ains and the tumultuous peaks of the Adirondacks, it stretched northward like an ocean—dark, vast.

"Isn't it lovely!" "Lovely!" "Lovely!" came like a refrain from a group of young girls.

"Out in our State," a neat, nervous Westerner remarked impartially to the seated people around him, "there's no such rough country as all this. The land is every bit *so*," pointing to a level grass field.

"You haven't such lakes, either," retorted a smart young lawyer from Plattsburg.

"Oh, we've lakes too," answered the Westerner. "But it's a fine body of water enough, is old Champlain."

Indeed, his braggadocio was plainly failing him. "I was a Burlington boy," we heard him tell a lady. "Never been back before." While that city grew at the east he stood up with folded arms. Presently he cried, "There's Dunder Rock!" and "There's Jupiter Island!" Then he asked, with a quaver in his voice, "If you'll just let me have that glass a minute? The University of Vermont ought to be right there. It stood on Main Street, with all the big buildings. Prettiest

street anywhere. Pretty as a Denver street.
Strange, I can't find it!" He sat down and
gripped the chair-arms. But, as roofs and
spires came swinging in to us, suddenly he
lurched forward, seized our little boy, lifted
him high, and shouted, " Ho, my lad, that's
Burlington! Ain't you tickled to see it?"

The child struggled away. There was a
general shoving back of chairs. But the
Westerner was down-stairs first, and, first,
strode over the gang-plank.

We followed *Gernegross* along the wharf
and into the little steamer *Chateaugay*.
There was no need now to ask, Whither
bound? Canoes filled the passageways, and
young men in knickerbockers and blazers
swarmed everywhere. One of these stopped
to give *Gernegross* a long, nautical stare,
then inquired pleasantly, " Ever been to the
Meet before?"

He and his wife were down from Canada.
They had reached camp yesterday, and to-
day had run up to Burlington for supplies.

" Last year we ate at the mess tent; this
year we are going to really camp out."

" Is there a great crowd?" we queried.
" Many ladies? What kind of people?"

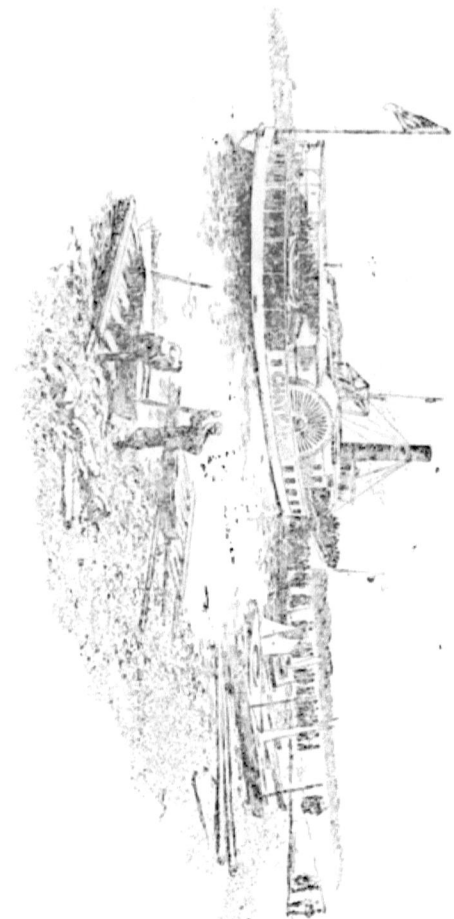

Landing

For the first time we faltered before that novel thing, now but a half - hour off — a Canoe Meet.

"All nice people—the whole three hundred," he said, smiling. "It is a fact; and it is odd, when the only condition of membership is the dollar fee. They are largely professional men, with a sprinkling of business men, and some mechanics. But they have one common bond—a genuine love of nature. Probably that accounts for the singular courtesy and congeniality—that, and the fact that so many bring their sisters and wives with them. I'll go and find my wife."

The lady he brought wore a bright, sashed boating costume, the cap well back on her fair hair for love of sunshine. To imagine her wearing anything less picturesque was impossible, with that free step, as though the winds upbuoyed her, and that large unconsciousness, as of nature itself. Blessed be a happy first impression! When Mrs. H—— held out her hand, and said, with a rich voice, and a smile that made the little phrase a new one, "Glad to meet you," the Canoe Meet took on, for us, romance it never lost.

" And were you never at a Meet before ?"
she said. " Oh, but I'm sure you will like
it ! It is the freest place in the world. You
can either be sociable and know everybody,
or you can go off and be alone, just as you
will. Isn't that so, Mr. H——?"

"Yes. They come for all sorts of reasons.
The women, mostly, to look pretty "—he
smiled at his wife; "the men, mostly, to
have a good time."

" That is what *you* say. But you know
very well that we Canadian girls come to
paddle, the same as yourselves."

And did she paddle alone, then ?

" Oh yes. I was brought up on the river.
Father taught us all to handle a boat the
first thing. You see, with us a canoe is
something different from what it is with
you States people. It is a means of com-
munication. Men go to business so, and to
the farms, and up into the wilderness to
hunt. Come, here we are."

But what magical new world was this?
what fairy fleet, flying about us in the wind
with long swallow-curves, or along the shore
with stroke of paddle darting in and out—
brilliant - hued, amber, crimson, pale and

5

dark green and blue—or drawn up on the
bowlder-strewn beach? what tents, far on
along the wooded bluff, each gleaming at the
head of its banner-hung cove? what picturesque inhabitants, welcoming the steamer?
now with call of nut-brown maid in her
canoe to some athlete striding along the
dock with boat on shoulder, now with a
cheer for a club marching ashore with its
great war-canoe. Ah, we understand; here
are the happy hunting-grounds! These are
the glorified braves!

"Does not the hotel interfere with all
this?" we asked Mrs. H——, as she led us
past the bulky, conventional structure on
the shore, to the grassy plain that covers
Willsborough Point, except for the rim of
woods.

"No; though it is full, too, with friends
of the canoists. But they are allowed in
camp only by special permit. This is the
mess pavilion. Those"—pointing to a collection of large tents and a row of flag-staffs
on a little knoll before us—"are Headquarters. They fly the States' flag, the English jack, the A. C. A., and some strings of
camp signals. And here is Squaw Point."

"What fairy fleet flying about us"

She parted the bushes, went along the be-
ginnings of a foot-path to the edge of the
bluff, and cried, " Welcome home !"

The tent, striped red, white, and blue, had
two chambers, tiny windows, and a board
floor continuing in a porch, whereon stood
a table and camp-chairs. She stepped within to give a womanly touch or two, and say,
" It will look better with the rugs we got in
Burlington."

" Squaw Point?" we said, with our eyes
upon the early lights of the city across the
lake, and the flushing cloud - Alps above.
" Then where is the bachelors' camp?"

" On the west, along Indian Bay. Except
the Toronto camp; that is at the north.
These beside us are Ottawa people." She
pointed to the next tent, whence some fair-
haired girls nodded back to her.

As she spoke, two canoes arrived with the
rest of our party and cargo. Our tent was
soon up. When the last rope was tied, Mr.
H—— appeared and said, " Now you will
come over and take tea with us."

While the dusk fell we talked of Canada,
to us a dim, romantic land. They thought
Canadians merrier than States people, and

"With stroke of paddle darting in and out"

more athletic. Mr. H—— himself had gone
nine hundred miles on Canadian rivers without once meeting a white man. The women
were healthier, they thought. They had no-
ticed it at the Meets. They paddled their
own boats, and in winter made long tramps
on snow-shoes.

Presently there was a sound of crackling
of wood and snapping sparks. Then a mandolin twanged, and a rich voice led in a jolly,
rhythmic song, with many voices catching
up the swinging refrain.

"I haven't heard so much laughter," said
one of our little party, musing in that im-
personal, abstract manner in which we lay
life as it is and as it has been beside the
spirit's promise of what it shall be—"I
haven't heard so much laughter since
I was a child and we were always laughing. They seem largely grown-up people. But they are not trying to be amusing
or amused. They laugh like children.
They have slipped back into childhood.
Listen!"

"Look!" cried some one else.

A light kindled in the west. It was in
silver along the mountain-tops. It sent

long, zigzag gleams across the lake to us. Then, lifting serene over the rim of the world, came the great, golden ball of the August full-moon.

VII

"While we poor sailors go skipping through the tops,
And the landlubbers lie down below, below, below."

THE merry voice drew on, passed with the stroke of paddles—ah, now we remembered! It was midmost of gondola days.

Hitherto the great lake had tantalized good sailors with light breezes. But this morning, when we looped back our tent after the night-long roar of trees and shout of waves, the broad blue was flecked with breakers.

"This would make glorious sailing for the trophy. Look!" as the cannon boomed, and across the sun's path came the usual morning procession to breakfast. "See the *Cricket* pass the *Mopsie*. The girl in the *Tempest* leads the line, as usual. But isn't it about time the boy was back from the grocery tent with the milk?"

"It's all those wicked cows," explained

"Victory or a ducking"

that person, appearing, heated, through the
trees. " I was almost here, when I saw them
going straight for the Headquarter's tent.
So I put the pail down, and went to chase
them. But they'd have been inside, sure, if
the Headquarter himself hadn't run out and
driven them away."

We sat to breakfast. A chipmunk above
us excitedly fed himself cedar buds with his
paws. Then the young captain of the *Dot*
sauntered through the woods whistling the
" Lorelei," and sat down on the moss to
discuss his failure in yesterday's race.

" It was such a beastly wind ; all cat's-
paws. What my rig wants is a good sociable big capful. Then my sail got jammed,
and I couldn't run it up as fast as the other
fellow. Did you see the pennant my sisters
worked for it ? A regular beauty ! But I
don't much care. My mother said, before
I came, she had prize-cups enough already
to keep bright. Here's a picture of the last
one, the —— cup, and the boat I took it
with." The boy passed on, whistling, frank
and gay and innocent.

" It is a pretty sight—that whole family of
young *Dot* interesting themselves so in his

canoing," we said, while, down on the beach, we exchanged morning greetings with the H.'s, and prepared to shove out in *Gerne-gross*.

"Yes. Probably they are glad to find one sport free from temptations to gambling, or objectionable company, or even the squandering of money. The father is a prominent New York business man, I happen to know. Though here we often meet a man for years without learning so much about him as his calling. The camp sentiment is, that canoing is common interest enough, and being here is sufficient passport."

We wondered where else, in our self-conscious society, a sentiment so unworldly could prevail.

"There's my Crusoe Cave!" exclaimed the little boy, pointing out a gap in the noble confusion of piled rocks we were passing, where the winter's gale showed still in the twisted and overhanging cedars. "It has the Magazine and all, perfect! I sit inside, and read *Robinson Crusoe*; and I'm going to read it there every day."

Boats! boats! boats! As we rounded the Point, now a launch puffed by, now a yacht

came tacking out; but chiefly and everywhere canoes were moving upon the water,
or lay along the beach of Indian Bay.
While for whilom dusky wigwams, a gala
village arranged by clubs fringed the woods.
" Brooklyn," " Lowell," " Holyoke," the flags
read, and over one group of small pyra-
midal brown tents was " Brown University."

Scraps of nautical conversation about
" builds " and " rigs " floated in upon us.
Beside one upturned boat knelt its owner,
surrounded by a group in dreadfully earnest
consultation.   On the next float a dignified
old gentleman stood trumpeting through his
hands, hot and excited as though at a po-
litical convention.   And the beau-ideal of a
dashing young sailor, in suit of white with
yellow kerchief knotted at the waist and
bared curls, flew shoreward to catch, from
the trumpet, " The leech draws a little,
Jack !"

" Watch the four in that birch-bark spring
to the leader's directions," said our Captain.
" I must ask what race is on next."

We stopped beside the familiar figure of
an artist, floating leisurely in a long canoe

that gleamed a dull yellow. *Hiawatha* was on the bow, and the legend,

> "And she floated on the water
> Like a yellow leaf in autumn,
> Like a yellow water-lily."

Some subtle likeness of expression between boat and man—was it a look of knowing how to penetrate to the inner joys of things?—prompted us to say, " Your boat always looks as though she were having good times, too."

He dropped his eyes, and responded, quietly, "She is my best friend."

He had expressed it for us all. There was no need to formulate it further, as this thin, ardent-faced girl, isolated in youth's haughty idealism, passed alone in her dark-red *Tempest;* or as *Mr. Micawber* drew beside us to read *Gernegross's* name and exchange notes on German travel, looking through his glasses for some humorous bit of life or adventure to "turn up."

"And yet they call us a wholly utilitarian people!" we began at dinner. But the rest was forgotten ; for that moment Mr. H.'s head appeared around the tent, and his voice said, "The Trophy race at two o'clock!"

When we paddled out the Point was black with people, huddling on bowlders, hemming the bluff, and scurrying about with glasses and cameras for "good points." And sixteen etherealized little boats—all wings and no body—moved out of Indian Bay manœuvring in a labyrinthine maze, and accompanied to the first buoy by a whole flotilla of spectators.

"Come on, ye little cockle-shells!" laughed the great tumbling lake, and the red and white buoys rose on the crests to beckon. The regatta committee steamed out, the stake-boat took its position, the cannon thundered.

"Go it, W——!" "J——'s ahead!" "No, its L——!" Calls, cheers, groans followed the fleet until the leading boats had drawn away from the rest. Then the spectators settled to the long watching.

"Where's B——?" asked a voice from the group with which we were interlocked, naming the son of a well-known general.

"His boat was broken just before the start."

"_Dreadfully earnest consultation_"

There was a murmur of disappointment; and the first speaker said: " I would like to see him win the trophy. He has done so much for canoing. And he is such a kind and unassuming fellow."

" Ha! Tom's over!" as one sail lay flat, righted, and came slowly ashore to receive a mock welcome.

" J——," said the yachting editor, with his glass on the expected winner, " is the greatest man I know for cutting clean around a buoy."

There was a breathless instant; for now that sailor came spinning in, lying far out to windward on his sliding seat, his feet strained against the coaming. His boat cut, rather than rode, the waves that, leaping, hid and drenched her, reeled around the buoy, gybed, and was off.

Conversation recommenced.

" Mr. S—— wants the ladies all to smile He has pointed his camera this way."

" Did you hear the joke on R——? You know he detests Visitors' Day; thinks the Association shouldn't have any. So the boys hung a sign before his tent—' Visitors welcome! Picnic here!' And when he

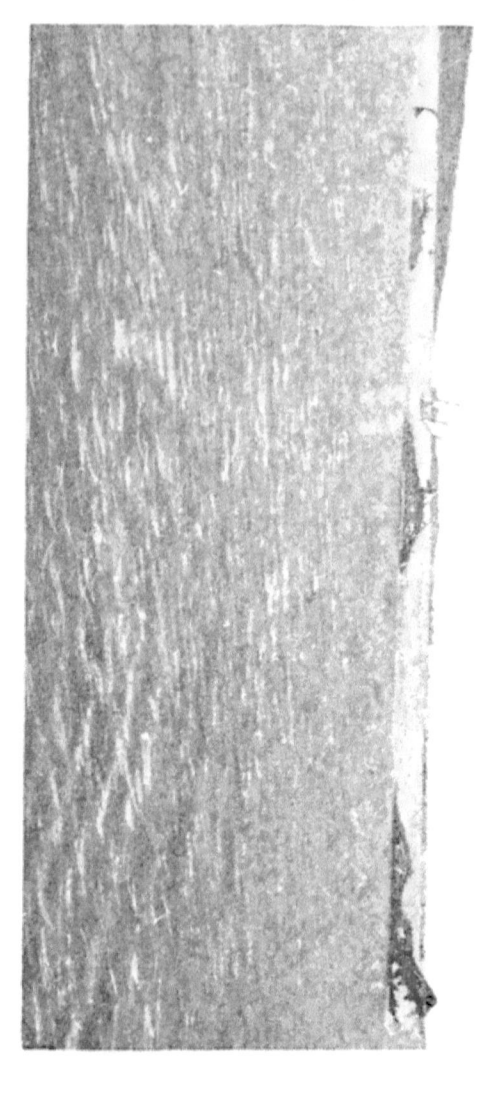

The Sea-serpent, Lake Champlain

came back, half a hundred people were under his awning !"

" Why doesn't he luff? He's making a fool of himself! There! He's let that fellow steal by to windward !"

Said an elderly German, " I am shust about to poobleesh my book on ze deescoovery of America by ze Irish."

" The Irish ? Good gracious !" exclaimed his nautical young friend. " And what was the man's name ?"

" I haf not yet *decided*."

A naughty convulsion of laughter threatened a capsize.

" I mean," explained the German gentleman, mildly, " dere are two names given. And I haf not yet *decided* which is ze most mythical."

Suddenly, from the depths of Indian Bay, a strange object advances, and calmly proceeds to round Willsborough Point—a monster, one hundred and fifty feet long, with gaping red jaws, pointed tail and crest—the fabled Champlain sea-serpent! As the idea dawns upon the astonished people they break into wild applause—al! except a poor little dog in one of the canoes, who yelps

with terror. The serpent gnashes its jaws.
Its scales glisten. It passes, surrounded by
admiring, harpoon-flinging crews. Mighty
laughter springs up before it, and dies slowly in its wake.

But the sun is sinking. And all eyes hang
on this one man, fleeting in to his last buoy,
beyond the power of the launch to accom-
pany him. He passes! And from sea
and shore comes one burst of gratulation.
"Three cheers for J——, the winner of
the trophy!" they greet him. He lifts his
cap. And another boat arriving, he
starts up, "Three cheers for the second
man!"

For delight of the little boy we paddle
out to the reef where lies the sea-serpent.
The mountains are lavender, and against
them glows Burlington. The city is hardly
seen by day. Then, at sunset, first a single
window flashes golden, like a humble great
soul found of its opportunity; and the rest
follow, and the leafage is vivid and the brick
warm. Quickly it fades to grayness; and
presently, and all night long, it is a serene
and solemn place of stars.

That same evening the signals on the

Reading "Robinson Crusoe"

tall flag-staff read, " At eight o'clock there
will be a general camp - fire in the ladies'
camp."

The moonlight, when it begins to glisten
on the meadow and to trickle into the woods,
reveals figures gathering with lanterns and
camp-chairs, mandolins and guitars. Below
the moon is the evening-star; and, below
that, the fire on the beach. The big logs
glow, and send slow sparks curling up like
serpents. Fireworks answer from Pumpkin
Reef. Cheers greet the winner of the trophy;
also the creator of the sea-serpent. " He
does get up the cleverest things! There
were the tableaux Monday night." " And
the water tournament." " And the procession of lanterns." The voices are merged
in the chorus, " While we were marching
through Georgia."

Which ended, a rollicking voice reels off
a Canadian dialect song:

A BALLAD OF LAKE CHAMPLAIN.

" 'Twas one dark night on Lac Champlain,
    An' de win' she's blow, blow, blow;
  When de crew of de wood-scow *Jule La Plante*
    Get scare an' run below.

For de win' she's blow like a hurricane;
  Bime-by she's blow some more;
An' de scow buss up on Lac Champlain,
  Juss half-mile from de shore.

" De cap'n she's walk de front deck;
  She's walk de hind deck too;
She's call de crew from up de hol';
  She's call de cook also.
Dat cook his name was Rosa,
  He's come from Montreal,
Was chamber-maid on a lumber barge
  On de big Lachine Canal.

" De win' she's blow from nor' eas' wes',
  An' de sous win' she's blow too;
When Rosa say, " Oh, capitan,
  Vatever s'all we do?"
De cap'n den she's trow de hank,
  But still dat scow she drif':
An' de crew he can't pass on dat shore,
  Because he's lose de skiff.

" De night vas dark like von black cat,
  An' de waves roll high an' fast:
Ven de cap'n take poor Rosa,
  An' she lash him to de mast.
Den de cap'n put on de life-preserve,
  An' she jump into de lac,
An' say, " Good-bye, my Rosa dear;
  I go drown for your sake."

" Nex' mornin' very hearly,
  'Bout half-past two, three, four,
De cap'n, cook, and wood-scow
  Lay corpses on dat shore.

For de win' she's blow like a hurricane;
  Bime-by she's blow some more;
An' de scow buss up on Lac-Champlain,
  'Bout half-mile from de shore.

" Now all you wood-scow sailor-mans
  Take warning by dat storm,
An' go an' marry von nice French girl,
  An' live on von nice farm.
Den de win' may blow like a hurricane,
  An' s'pose she's blow some more,
You von't get drown on Lac Champlain,
  So long you stay on shore."

Stories follow. College songs fill in the pauses. Armfuls of hemlock boughs, heaped upon the fire, crackle in accompaniment. Now there is a call for ——, and a rich voice sings to the mandolin a bit of melodious sentimentalism that, combined with the light of moon and stars and the gloom of sea and shore, distracts all susceptible youths and maidens, and discovers softness in the sturdiest of bachelors and in the most pro-saic of married people :

" I want no kingdom where thou art, Love;
  I want no throne to make me blest.

" I need not fear, whate'er betide me,
  For straight and sweet my pathway lies;
I want no stars in heaven to guide me
  While I gaze in your dear eyes."

Around the Camp-fire

Then, gathering up all chords, the voice
leads into "America" and "God save the
Queen," and so to good-night.

Gondola days cannot last forever.

A few evenings later there was a gathering at Headquarters, when the prizes were
awarded—the Pecowsic and Commodore's
cups, the beautiful trophy, the flags and pen-
nants—and when the outgoing Commodore
made his farewell speech, and the incom-
ing one was welcomed with the call of the
A. C. A.

Afterwards we crossed the meadows to
look for the last time into Indian Bay. Still
there came up the tinkle of guitars, sing-
ing, laughter, dip of paddles. But the tents
were few. Many boats lay dismantled. Now
lines of light stole between the shadows of
the shores.

We turned. The August moon was on
the wane.

VIII

WE rarely expect the charm of a journey to extend to the return. And if the old route must be retravelled, we feel impatient of it as of some worn-out thing that persists in existing. But as we go our way, we discover that this return may be richest in the very quality which we denied to it— in novelty. For places seen before have a way of turning upon us wholly new looks.

We left Willsborough Point with farewells called from the scattered tents along the shore. The familiar lake was heartlessly unaware of us—was soon positively unkind with wind and rain; so that we put in at Essex.

Once a bustling port, now the town was picturesquely dull, and *Gernegross* made a great stir there. People ran to factory windows and down streets, and stood compacted around the dock. And when our Cap-

Paddling Indian Canoes with Single Blade

tain called up, " Where is the best place
to land ?" a regiment of boys and men ran
to give a practical reply.

We waited for the steamboat in company
with a party of farmer folk, the women
very natural and lovable in old-fashioned
gowns and bonnetfuls of preposterous buttercups and poppies. " Come again ?" one
of them answered a friend who was seeing
her off. " Well, I never before found the
time when I could get away, and I don't expect to again in a hurry." When the steamboat landed them across the lake, we saw
them swallowed up in bulging top-wagons,
and their sweet thin faces duly set towards
their devouring farms. Then we recrossed
to Westport, and in the dark found a hotel.

It was filled with the race of summer
boarders. We had glimpses of them on
stiff chairs and sofas around the parlor
walls. A lady at the piano was asking,
" What are the wild waves saying ?" and a
gentleman was giving an energetic, but, as
we thought, incorrect answer with the cor-
net. In the intervals of the entertainment
a baby cried in the wing. Presently a blond
young woman, with a book under her arm.

passed our window, in company with a
young man in a red blazer. " Das est ein—
no, eine—Fräulein, isn't it?" said she. Then,
as they reached the end of the path, " Wie
heissen sie ein gate?" It looked a compre-
hensive way of studying German, and ful-
of possibilities for the young man in the red
blazer, as the eager blond young woman
should advance in her vocabulary.

The next morning we put off into the
shining bay, watched by the senile old gaffer.
" Well, well! Seen the lake all my life, but
I've never seen sich a thing as this! So that
is a canoe? Thought they were like the
dugouts we used to have in my young days.
Now I can say I've seen one. Ha, ha!
hum!"

Down at Mr. Thorp's point we were welcomed like old friends. And the lake being
now tempestuous, we camped in the grove
for several days, while the little boy sailed
cucumber boats with the Thorp children.
Surely it is vain to ransack the earth for
costly amusements for children. Our little
boy counts as the chief delight of the trip
the sailing of these cucumber boats and the
towing of his mother on the canal.

Stranded

When we did start out, the bay by Port Henry rose into a furious sea, and drove us upon the beach at Crown Point. We lunched at the ruined fort, with a picnic party not interesting to us until we met them again at the light-house. They were preparing to return to Ticonderoga in a tub of a launch which took on, for us, positive beauty.

"Could you give us a tow?" asked our Captain.

"Goes too fast."

"Could you—take us on board?"

They thought they could. Quickly the bargain was made and we were seated at the bow, and steaming between banks we had once thought far apart, but which now, after the broad upper lake, seemed very near. The party behind us waxed merry over their baskets and paper bags. They sang "Over the Summer Sea" and "Beloved Eye, beloved Star," and others of the maudlin songs that constitute the music of many of our people. Meanwhile the sun gilded the little clouds about him, and set them sailing in pale green lakes, and made the trees along the hill-tops look like lace-work against the gold. Then night settled upon

the shores, and in darkness we landed at
Fort Ticonderoga.

We stumbled up to the Heights of Carillon.   There was no genial Professor now ;
only his tent-poles, which we proceeded to
use.   The winds were true to us.   Fasci-
nated, we heard them gather to their all-
absorbing shout.   But we had no second
adventure.

The next day was our last on Lake Champlain.   Hour after hour we went along the
winding creek which constitutes the upper
lake, following the red-and-black beacons
that show the way among the rushes.
Flocks of red-winged starlings made their
evolutions over our heads, with pretty
showings of their bright epaulets.

At Whitehall we met the canal.   That
was on a wash-day.   The canal-boat women
were on deck to receive us, and the clothes
on the lines flapped like flags.   Some of our
old friends recognized us, and were curious
as to where we had been, and received smil-
ingly our Captain's fine answer, " Oh, everywhere !"

It had been mowing-time as we came up.
Now the threshing-machines were at work,

A War Canoe

and the loads of grain and the yellow stacks of sheaves looked like the pictures labelled "Harvesting." The wild flowers, too, were changed. The varying tints of the asters were shot through with damask spires of sumac berries. And when we towed, clouds of yellow butterflies rose at our feet.

At last we reached Albany. At sight of its houses, all the commonplace wants of civilized man suddenly awoke in us—for a house and a bed and tables and chairs and things. We met some of our camp acquaintances—young business men of the Mohican Club, who told us of their beautiful club-house a little below on the river, whither they paddle of evenings in their war canoe, and invited us to take possession of it for the night. But now we were upon a stampede. We even fled dastardly from *Gernegross*, leaving her on board the river steamboat; and took to the cars.

And, rushing southward through the evening, we laughed to think how we would steal a march upon our friends; creep home through the darkness by back ways, and appear in the morning neat, conventionalized, innocent of ever having camped out.

7

But as we alighted at the station, it was thronged with people. Music and jubilation filled the air. Bonfires burned on every corner, and every one we knew and did not know was out upon the pavement.

So every journey is rich in the unexpected, and the greatest surprise of all may await us at the end. What if this be also true of that other journey upon which we are all trudging together? What and if, for even the shabbiest traveller — the one who, foot-sore, asks only rest at the end — there shall be, and this time not unaware of him, the royalest of welcomes?

ADDENDA

CAMPING is not for every one. It is not for the dear finnicky souls whom the very thought of disorder upsets, whose living must always be as decorous and as planned as the garden of Mistress Mary,

> "With cockle-shells and silver bells,
> And cowslips all arow."

The Club-house

It is not for the women to whom a tangle of deep grass means a possible snake. It is not for the men whose appetite fails them at a table less than three feet above grasshoppers and crickets. It is not for people of few resources, miserable when alone.

It is for all who are in love with Nature, who desire to know her in every mood—in storm, in the wilderness, in the night, and, with Keats,

> " Far, far away to leave
> All meaner thoughts, and take a sweet reprieve
> From little cares:"

who, away from the shows of things, find clearer judgments sifting down between the leaves with the sunlight and springing up with the grass-blades ; and who are willing to pay for all this the price of some sacrifice of ease and order and conventionality.

To those about to attempt it for the first time, especially if they intend combining it with economy, a few simple hints from our own experience of camping may be helpful.

Our tent is the least troublesome and the most serviceable we have seen. It is made

of unbleached muslin, without seams; the
bottom sewed in, and bordered by an oiled
cotton rope made into loops for its six pegs.
In its bag with all its ropes it makes a pack-
age two feet by ten inches, and weighs nine
pounds. To pitch it we peg the floor in
position, throw the ridge-rope over two con-
venient tree limbs, straighten out the rear
wall by its three guys, stretch ventilators,
pull up the sag of the roof by a cord attach-
ed to a loop in the centre—and are ready
for fair weather or foul. The perpendicular
front closes it by night, and is stretched out
as an awning by day. A loose flounce, six
inches wide, sewed around the tent four
inches from the bottom, is very important
for preventing the soaking in of water under
the floor. The whole is water-proofed by
the alum sugar-of-lead process, and has
never leaked.

Clothing should be all of flannel, with an
extra jacket, and not a superfluous article.

For our party of three we carried an extra
heavy copper-bottomed three-quart pail
with cover, and a removable chain handle;
a second pail of the same kind fitting into
the first; and within this five deep tin

basins, three tin cups, three small steel
knives and forks, and ten dessert-spoons.
Unbleached muslin cases made with drawing strings covered both pails. The axe,
broiler, and frying-pan, all very small, had a
muslin bag to themselves. In addition we
had a tiny alcohol lamp costing thirty cents,

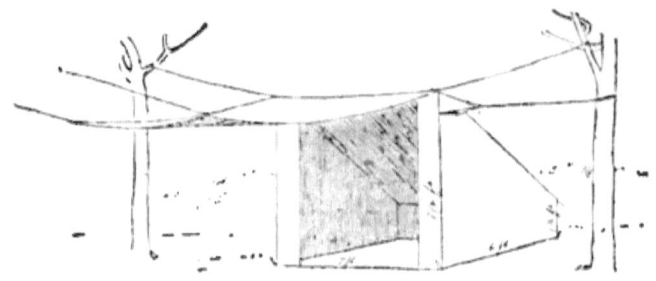

Diagram of Tent

and a can of wood alcohol for use inside the
tent, or when in haste ; also a chain for
hanging pails over a wood-fire. Safety-
matches were a great convenience in rain or
wind.

It is hardly necessary to say that camp
cookery will usually be of the simplest.
The compensation lies in the vigorous appetite of the camper. Canned goods are

always procurable. Farm - houses may be depended upon for bread and butter, milk and eggs, fruit and vegetables. Oatmeal and coffee serve as the basis of breakfast. At noon a cold lunch is easiest. It is best to camp by four o'clock in the afternoon at the latest, and have plenty of time for preparing dinner.

It is often restful to spend a night or rainy day at a farm-house. The people in quiet regions are hospitable, and glad to meet strangers. There should be no spirit of haste in the journey. The best plan is to go but a few miles a day, and to make frequent and often long halts. If one must hurry, let it be by railroads and steamboats.

A suitable canoe is of the highest importance. It should be light and swift, yet capable of carrying a good load and of enduring rough usage. Such a craft our Canadian friends have fashioned after the Indian "birch-bark," the famous *Peterborough*, so called from the town of its builder, William English. This canoe seems to be the model, both in form and construction, for all the North country. With its high curving ends, it is a beautiful boat, often fancifully painted with gay Indian designs. And especially when a lady paddles with the single blade, kneeling Indian fashion, supported by the round hollow thwart, the grace and movement render the whole the prettiest picture that floats.

No woman ought to venture far from shore in such a boat, or to use a sail—except, perhaps, a small square sail at the bow, to take advantage of a favoring breeze. The true canoist is a frequenter of forest waterways, and loves best to float with the stream.

For convenience in loading and unloading, it is well to have the luggage arranged in eight or ten separate packages, all easy to pick up and handle. A bag is serviceable for extra clothing, a very light box for provisions; another smaller box, containing everything likely to be needed while in the camp, should be carried within easy reach. The packing is done on shore, the luggage covered by a piece of water-proof cloth, either tucked in or fastened around screwheads under the outer edge of the gunwale.

One will, of course, carry a camera with which to preserve, and to multiply for

friends, the delights of the trip.   Many
" snap-shooters," however, bring home commonplace collections of photographic mem-
orabilia rather than pictures. For the latter,
some knowledge of pictorial effect in pho-
tography is necessary.   Read a good book
on the subject, and secure the criticism of
any intelligent photographer upon some
good or bad pictures and upon some pre-
liminary attempts of your own. We followed
the advice of a master of the art, and are
the fortunate owners of a " Henry Clay "
camera. This takes 5-by-7 pictures, and
has a wide range of devices for securing
complete pictorial results.

A few simple medicines are indispensable.
These are best carried in highly concentrat-
ed forms.   But our stand-bys are aromatic
spirits of ammonia, and collodion.

As to reading we would recommend one
book apiece—a book that can be read and
read again—for days too hot to travel, or
rainy days, or the Sabbath.   More even an
inveterate bookworm will find in the way—
a temptation to lose much of the advantage of such a trip.

For the delights of canoing come from

nature and meditation, and the odd and novel incidents of the journey. It is a noble pleasure, worthy to grow, as it rapidly does, in favor, and to characterize our American people.

www.ingramcontent.com/pod-product-compliance
Lightning Source LLC
Chambersburg PA
CBHW020235030726
47497CB00009B/3111